Mr. Wink and His Shadow, Ned

by Dick Gackenbach

Harper & Row, Publishers

For Murray and Marvin

Library of Congress Cataloging in Publication Data
Gackenbach, Dick.
    Mr. Wink and his shadow, Ned.

    Summary: After a silly tiff, Mr. Wink decides to find
a new shadow.
    [1. Shadows—Fiction]   I. Title.
PZ7.G117Mr 1983   [E]   82-47711
ISBN 0-06-021969-6
ISBN 0-06-021974-2 (lib. bdg.)

First Edition

Short Mr. Wink and his tall shadow, Ned, had
good times together. Sometimes they made
animal shadows on the wall.

Sometimes they raced each other up and down
the sidewalk.

And some days they would take long pleasant
walks in the park together.

But there were times when Ned and Mr. Wink,
like most good friends, would have a tiff about
something silly.

When Mr. Wink raked his garden, Ned would rake in front of him. "Get out of my way," Mr. Wink would shout at Ned. "I can't see what I'm doing."

If Mr. Wink wished to relax and read by the fire,
Ned wanted to dance on the walls. "Sit down and
be still," Mr. Wink would yell. "I'm trying to read."

And late at night, when Mr. Wink opened the refrigerator door, Ned would jump up behind him and frighten Mr. Wink out of his wits.

"Ha!" Ned would laugh and tease. "Mr. Wink is afraid of his own shadow!"

But what really upset Mr. Wink was that Ned
disappeared every time it rained!

"Ned, where are you?" he called out as he
searched for his shadow in garbage cans, under
rugs, and in every dresser drawer. "Where does
that shadow go?"

As long as it rained, and the clouds covered the
sun, Mr. Wink could not go outside and race with
Ned, or take their pleasant walks together.

"Oh, how I hate rainy days," Mr. Wink would grumble. "I have no one to keep me company." Mr. Wink was lonesome. He sat by the window hour after hour, hoping for the sun to shine, and wishing Ned would come home.

After one very gloomy day, Mr. Wink could bear it no longer. "Why do you leave me?" he yelled at Ned. "Just where do you go when it rains?"

"Sorry," Ned told him. "It's a secret! Only a shadow knows."

"Oh, so!" snapped Mr. Wink. "It's all right to play games with me, or take walks with me, or even scare the wits out of me in the middle of the night, but I'm not good enough for you to share a secret with."

"It's not that," replied Ned. "It's because every shadow has taken an oath never to tell."

"Oh, please tell me," Mr. Wink pleaded.

"No!" said Ned.

Mr. Wink was angry. "I demand to know," he said, stamping his foot.

"I'll never tell," said Ned, firmly. "And that's final!"

"Okay," said Mr. Wink. "If that's the way you want to be, I'll find a new shadow. A short one that suits me better!"

"And I," said Ned, "will find someone new, too, someone with less of a temper."

"Fine with me!" said Mr. Wink, turning his back on Ned.

"Fine with me!" said Ned, slamming the door as he left.

After that Ned searched everywhere for someone else to follow around. He tried to shadow a dog, even a car. Nothing wanted another shadow hanging around.

Ned even went to the baby ward at the
hospital. Perhaps, he thought, something as new
as a baby would need a shadow.

"No, I'm sorry," a nurse told Ned, "babies
come complete with their own shadows."

15

Tired and lonely, Ned was ready to swallow his pride and ask Mr. Wink to take him back. But then he saw a sign that made him change his mind.

"COME TO FLORIDA, WHERE THE SUN ALWAYS SHINES!" it said.

"Of course," Ned cried out. "That's where I'll go. With so much sun, shadows must be needed there."

A short time later,
and with a little bit of luck,
Ned was riding comfortably
in the shadow of a balloon
headed for Florida.

Mr. Wink had been having his troubles too! He felt strange without a shadow following him around.

He tried to paint a shadow, but when Mr. Wink ran down the street, the painted shadow did not move.

"Ned would have raced after me," said Mr. Wink, sadly.

Mr. Wink tied a long dark sheet to his ankles,
but the sheet tangled in his feet and he fell down.
"Oh my," said Mr. Wink. "Ned never made me
fall."

Mr. Wink went to the circus. Perhaps, he thought, the Fat Lady or the Tall Man would share part of their big shadows with him.

"Certainly not," said the Fat Lady.

"I can't spare an inch of mine," said the Tall Man.

If only he had never quarreled with Ned, Mr. Wink wished as he walked back home. He was certain he would never have a shadow again. Then he saw a sign that cheered him up.

"COME TO FLORIDA, WHERE THE SUN ALWAYS SHINES!" he read.

"What a great idea!" Mr. Wink cried. "There must be extra shadows in such a sunny place."

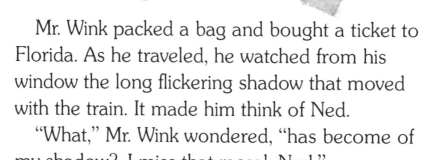

Mr. Wink packed a bag and bought a ticket to Florida. As he traveled, he watched from his window the long flickering shadow that moved with the train. It made him think of Ned.

"What," Mr. Wink wondered, "has become of my shadow? I miss that rascal, Ned."

Mr. Wink found all kinds of shadows in Florida,
but not one extra one to spare for him.

"What now?" he said to himself. "Where shall I
look next?"

Then, as often happens in Florida, a fierce rain
blew in from the sea. Everyone on the beach ran
for cover beneath the awning of a taco stand.

Soon the storm passed. Everyone under the awning went back to sit in the sun, or play in the sand.

Everyone, that is, except the downhearted Mr. Wink and one lonely, tall shadow.

The man and the shadow took a long look at one another. It was the shadow who spoke first. "Could that be my own ill-tempered Mr. Wink?"

"And could that be my own troublesome shadow, Ned?" was the reply.

"It's me!" shouted Ned.

"It's me too!" cried Mr. Wink.

Just like long-lost friends, they hugged and patted each other, and when the excitement was over, Mr. Wink said, "Please come home. I can't wait to play animal shadows on the wall again."

"And I can't wait to race you down the street again," said Ned. "But I *will* always have to leave you when it rains, and I can never tell you why."

"That's fine with me," agreed Mr. Wink. "I'd rather be without a shadow on rainy days than never have a shadow at all."

"We *do* make a good team," said Ned. "Let's go home."

Although they still had silly quarrels from time to time, Ned and Mr. Wink never parted company again. Except, of course, on rainy days.

316462   P27.G117   OK cuu